For my two moms.
– Adam

Climb a Giraffe written by Adam Ciccio and illustrated by Yuke Li

ISBN 978-1-60537-649-3

This book was printed in August 2021 at Nikara, M. R. Štefánika 858/25, 963 01 Krupina, Slovakia.

First Edition
10 9 8 7 6 5 4 3 2 1

Clavis Publishing supports the First Amendment and celebrates the right to read.

WRITTEN BY ADAM CICCIO
ILLUSTRATED BY YUKE LI

CLIMB A
GIRAFFE

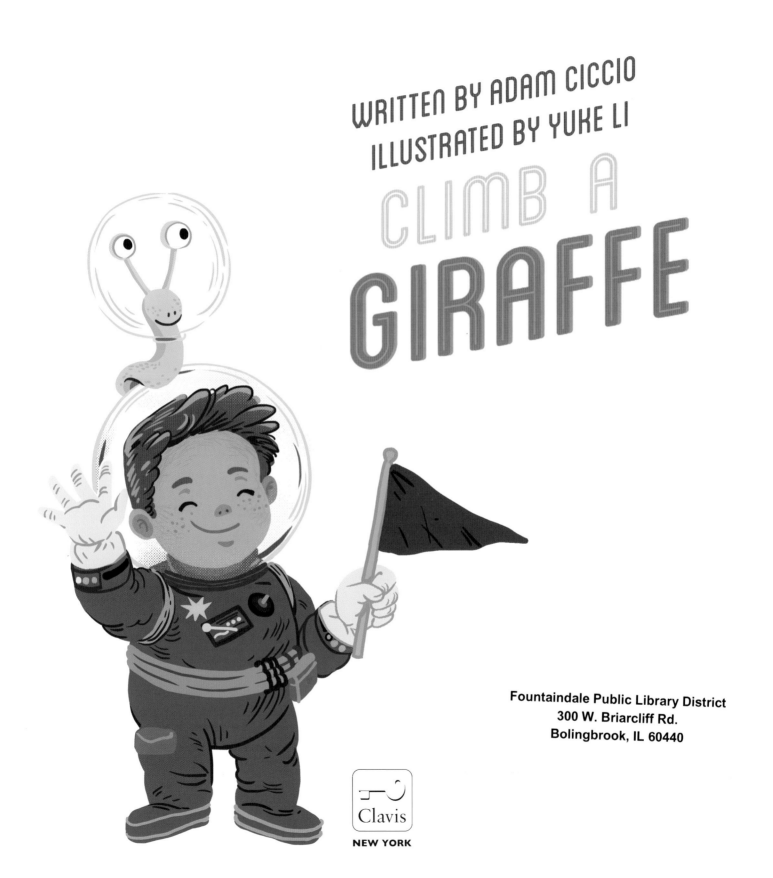

Fountaindale Public Library District
300 W. Briarcliff Rd.
Bolingbrook, IL 60440

Clavis

NEW YORK

A kid like me hears a lot of rules . . .

"Don't go in there."

"Don't do that!"

"Walk in a straight line."

"Sit crisscross on the mat."

The truth is . . .

I want to climb a giraffe.

I'll see the world from up high.

I want to dance with a peacock.
She can teach me how to fly!

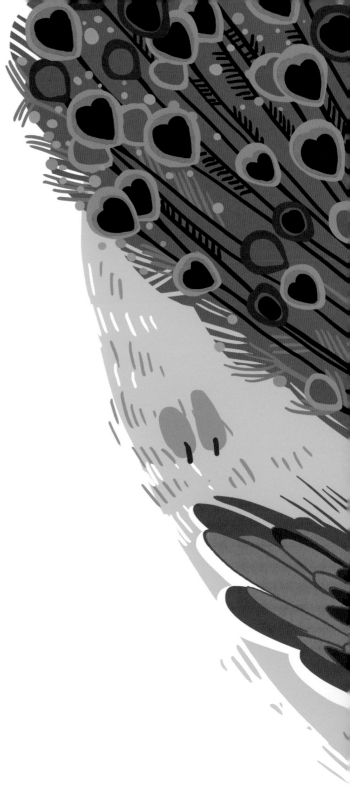

I promise I'll look both ways.

I won't stare at the sun.

I'll eat all my vegetables . . .
for my long journey of fun.

I'll dig for lost treasure.
And find a slimy slug.

I'll name him Geronimo. He's the world's first explorer bug!

We'll build a rocket ship.
And make sure we can both fit.

I'll sit in the front.

Geronimo, where do you want to sit?

I'll make sure to make my bed . . .

when I build my house on Mars.

Because rules are good . . .
but adventure is too.

I'll always explore beyond the horizon.
And hopefully, so do you!